KUMAK'S RIVER

A Tall Tale from the Far North

MICHAEL BANIA

Alaska Northwest Books®

*E*ach spring the frozen river near Kumak's house cracked and broke into millions of pieces. But this year the pieces of ice were bigger than anyone in Kumak's family could remember. Chunks of ice as big as houses crashed into each other and started moving downriver on their way to the sea.

While Kumak and his family stood listening to the ice scrape along the riverbanks, Kumak said, "As sure as seagulls return in spring, that river will come to visit us today."

Soon enough, the ice jammed in a bend of the river. Kumak's dogs leaped up and down, barking as the huge chunks of ice piled onto each other and came to a stop.

Then, just as Kumak said, the river came to visit.

First the water spilled out of the riverbanks. It flowed up over the sandy beach and inched its way past the fish racks and caches. Then the water rose higher, climbing toward the houses where the villagers lived.

"Here it comes!" shouted Kumak's wife as water swirled past the church steps.

"Good thing we put our dried fish and meat in the cache last fall," said Kumak's wife's mother as the river rose even higher, surging past the store.

"Hooray! No classes today!" shouted Kumak's sons and daughters as the icy water surrounded the school.

But it didn't stop there. It continued rising toward all the houses of the village.

Kumak and his family scrambled up on top of their house.

Kumak pushed his wife up.

He pushed his wife's mother up.

He pushed his sons and daughters up.

But before Kumak himself climbed up, he put all
his dogs into the family boat and tied it to the house.

"Just in time!" said Kumak.
"Just in time!" said his family as
they pulled Kumak up.

No sooner had the villagers scrambled to their
rooftops, than the river surrounded them all!
"*Just in time!*" they said.

It was a warm and sunny day. No one needed
a jacket or gloves. People sat on their houses
and shouted across to their neighbors.
"How are you doing?" they called.

"We're doing fine," their neighbors called back.

Even though the ice was no longer moving, smaller chunks sometimes broke away from the main river and floated toward the houses.

With a long pole, Kumak pushed away any ice that came too close.

The village dogs sat in their boats
waiting for something to happen.

Then something *did* happen.
While Kumak's family sat on top of their house,
the river down below went wherever it wanted to go.
And it did whatever it wanted to do.

"Look!" said Kumak's wife. At one o'clock the river began pushing all the oil drums away.

"Look!" said Kumak's wife's mother.
At two o'clock the river was busy shoving all
the net floats and fish tubs away.

"Look!" said Kumak's sons and daughters. At three o'clock the river stole all the children's toys and pulled them away.

"Oh no!" wailed Kumak's sons and daughters, as they watched their playthings drift by. "We will never see our toys again!"

"What can we do?" said Kumak pushing away
another chunk of ice. "A river does what a river does."

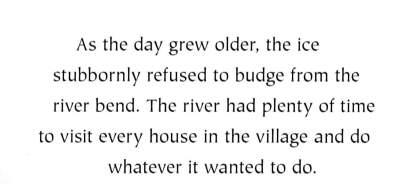

As the day grew older, the ice
stubbornly refused to budge from the
river bend. The river had plenty of time
to visit every house in the village and do
whatever it wanted to do.

While Kumak and his family sat and waited, enormous
pressure was building up behind the ice jam. More and more
ice from upriver kept coming downriver, pushing toward the sea.
With no place to go, the ice jam grew bigger and bigger and bigger. . .

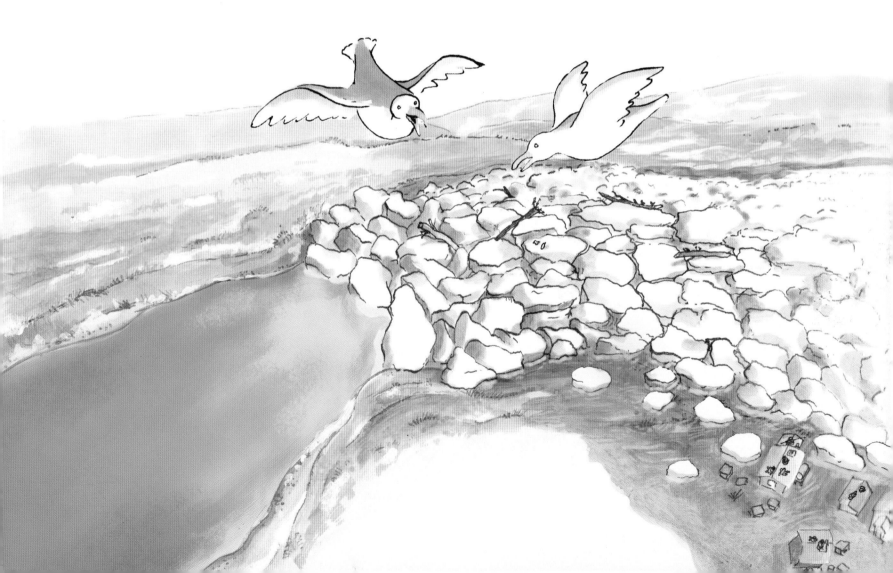

At four o'clock sharp, the ice finally broke free. The river surged forward tossing ice and logs into the air.

Just like someone pulled a plug in a bathtub, the water around the village started going down.

"Hooray!" everyone shouted with joy.

The water swooshed away from their houses. It splashed by the school, sloshed past the store and the church steps. It swirled around the fish racks and caches. And finally the water slid down over the sandy beach, back into the riverbanks where it belonged.

"*Just in time!*" cried the villagers, as they jumped down from their rooftops. Whatever they had not tied down before the flood, the river had carried away.

Kumak and his family searched around their house. Sure enough there were no oil drums, no fish tubs or net floats, and no toys.

Kumak's wife called to their neighbors, "Have you seen our oil drums, fish tubs, net floats, or toys?"

Their neighbors called back, "No, ours are missing too."

And when Kumak looked at the spot where he had tied the boat holding his dogs, they were gone!

"We will never see our dogs again," wailed Kumak's sons and daughters.

Kumak gathered his family. "The river took our things and it took our neighbors' things. It had its turn to do what it wanted to do. Now it is time for us to do what we need to do."

Kumak and his family began searching the village for their missing things.

At five o'clock, Kumak heard a neighbor call out, "We hear barking at Uncle Buggy's house!" Like frisky caribou, everyone ran to Uncle Buggy's house. There they found a few dogs, but not Kumak's dogs.

They also found all their oil drums and happily rolled them back home.

At six o'clock, Kumak heard another neighbor call out, "We hear barking at Taata Joe's house!" Like playful seals, the villagers splashed to Taata Joe's house. There they found more dogs, but still not Kumak's dogs.

Happily, they did find all the missing net floats and fish tubs, which they untangled and carried home.

"Where are our toys and our dogs?" sniffed Kumak's children. "Did the ice carry them away?" But Kumak couldn't say. Perhaps the river had carried them out to sea. Kumak and his family ran from house to house, up and down the muddy roads, searching all along the river. But they found no dogs and no toys.

At seven o'clock, just as everyone was taking a break for dinner, a neighbor knocked on Kumak's door. "We hear howling at Auntie Rosie's house!"

Leaping up, Kumak and his family joined the villagers and ran like the wind through the willows to Auntie Rosie's house. There they spotted an enormous pile of toys. But where were Kumak's dogs?

"Here they are!" cried Little Nate.

"*Just in time!*" cheered the villagers.
"*Just in time,*" said Kumak's family.

At the end of the very long day, all the missing things were back where they belonged. The village children raced along the edge of the river watching the last of the ice go out.

"That river was a big help this year," said Kumak. "And it didn't visit for too long."

"Now it will bring us fish and seals," said Kumak's wife.

"Now we can travel to camp and pick berries," said Kumak's wife's mother. It had been eight long months since the river was free of ice. Everyone was eager to get out on the water again.

"Now it is our turn to visit the river," said Kumak.

"Let's go boating!" the children shouted.

"Yes! Let's go boating," cried the villagers.

And so they did.

Author's Note

Spring breakup is a happy time for every one who lives in the remote villages of Northwest Alaska. As the arctic winter fades away, the increasing sunlight brings dramatic changes.

Buckland, the village where I lived and taught, sits at a bend in the Buckland River. Each year as the days grow longer, spring "breakup" occurs. The river ice cracks apart and moves downriver toward the sea. It is a rare year that ice does not jam up in a bend. Some years when the ice is especially thick, or unusually hot weather causes it to break up suddenly, severe flooding occurs.

When my son was three years old, our family experienced one of these floods. It was a hot May day and the rising water soon flowed into the whole town. Small boats became floating doghouses. And while school was canceled for the students, the principal drove his boat to each teacher's house and picked us up for work.

Most people stay put to protect their homes and belongings. Those closest to the river climb onto their rooftops and push stray ice chunks away. Fortunately, most houses, like Kumak's, are built on stilts to keep them dry. When the river finally goes down it takes a lot of cooperation to locate everyone's missing belongings.

One of the most important Iñupiaq values is "Respect for Nature." The Iñupiat are used to these yearly floods and accept them as a way of life. With everyone helping each other, life quickly returns to normal. As soon as the ice goes out, people drive their boats on the river collecting driftwood or simply having fun.

In spring the sun doesn't set until late at night, so there are many hours to enjoy the river. By early June, the sun won't set at all for six weeks. After the long, cold winter, when the river is frozen over for eight months, the ice-free water is a welcome sight.

Kumak = KOO-muk

For Rosie, who was my teacher while we were teaching the children.
In celebration of breakup, one of the best days of the year!

Text and illustrations © 2012
by Michael Bania

First printing 2012

Alaska Northwest Books®
An imprint of Graphic Arts Books
P.O. Box 56118
Portland, OR 97238-6118
(503) 254-5591

www.graphicartsbooks.com

Library of Congress Cataloging-in-Publication Data
Bania, Michael, 1944-
    Kumak's river : a tall tale from the Far North / Michael
Bania.
        p. cm.
ISBN 978-0-88240-886-6 (hardbound : alk. paper) — ISBN
978-0-88240-887-3 (softbound : alk. paper)
    1. Inuit—Alaska—Juvenile fiction. I. Title.
PZ7.B2145Kw 2004
[E]—dc23
                                        2012019726

Editor: Michelle McCann

Printed in China